The Marvelous Mind of Matthew McGhee, Age 8

Master of Minds?

To Suanne Smith Jones and
Cecily Cunningham Morris —S. W.

To Samantha and Carter —A. C.

First Aladdin Paperbacks edition February 2004

Text copyright © 2004 by Suzanne Williams
Illustrations copyright © 2004 by Abby Carter

ALADDIN PAPERBACKS
An imprint of Simon & Schuster
Children's Publishing Division
1230 Avenue of the Americas
New York, NY 10020

Designed by Sammy Yuen Jr.
The text of this book was set in Century ITC.

Printed in the United States of America
2 4 6 8 10 9 7 5 3 1

Library of Congress Control Number 2003106059

ISBN 0-689-86336-5

The Marvelous Mind of Matthew McGhee, Age 8,

Master of Minds?

By Suzanne Williams
Illustrated by Abby Carter

Aladdin Paperbacks
New York London Toronto Sydney

Chapter One

Wishful Thinking

"**P**lease pass your homework papers forward," said Matthew's third-grade teacher, Ms. White.

Matthew pawed frantically through his backpack.

Daniel tapped Matthew on the shoulder. Sandy-haired, with lots of freckles, Daniel shared a double desk with Matthew.

Rolling his eyes, Daniel said, "Why do you even bother to search? You know you didn't do it." Then Daniel passed *his* homework to the person ahead of him.

"Maybe I did, and just forgot that I did," said Matthew. But even as he said it, he knew it wasn't true. It was what his mother called "wishful thinking." And as she often told him, "Wishful thinking solves nothing." Matthew did a lot of wishful thinking.

"Too bad you'll have to stay after school again," said Daniel. "I was going to ask you over this afternoon to play ball with Tim and Jess and me."

Matthew sighed. "Maybe I could come over a little later."

"Sorry," said Daniel. "I only have an hour to play. I have to go somewhere with my mom later on."

"Well, thanks anyway," said Matthew. Last year, in second grade, he and Daniel had been best friends. But lately Daniel played more with Tim and Jess. It was just Matthew's luck that the last few times Daniel had asked him to play, he couldn't.

At the end of the day Matthew waited for Ms. White to call his name and ask him to stay and finish his missing homework. He'd meant to do it last night. He *always* meant to do it. But thoughts of homework seemed to vanish like puffs of smoke once he was home.

Just once, Matthew wished Ms. White would forget about his missing homework. He squeezed his eyes shut. *Let Matthew go. Let Matthew go,* he thought at his teacher. Maybe it was just wishful thinking, but what could it hurt?

"Matthew?"

He opened his eyes. Ms. White stood over his desk. All the other kids had left. Ms. White frowned. "Do you *enjoy* staying here after school every day?"

Matthew stared up at her. Was this a trick question? Slowly, he shook his head no.

Ms. White sighed, then glanced at her watch. "I'm not sure why I'm doing this, but I'm going to let you go. Keeping you after school doesn't seem to help anyway. Just don't forget, you'll have *two* homework assignments to complete tonight."

Matthew couldn't believe his ears. "Thanks, Ms. White. I won't forget!" He jumped up, grabbed his backpack, and headed for the door. He turned as he reached the door. "Bye," he said.

Ms. White gave him a tired wave of her hand.

Chapter Two

Rebecca

Matthew headed for Daniel's house. He'd hoped to catch up with Daniel, Tim, and Jess, but they were nowhere in sight. No matter. If he walked fast, he could be at Daniel's in ten minutes. Then he'd still have most of an hour to play ball.

It was certainly nice of Ms. White to let him go. Especially since Matthew wasn't at all sure she really liked him. Every time she looked at him she either frowned or sighed.

Ms. White was stricter than any teacher Matthew had ever had when it came to assignments and homework. Why *had* she let him go today? Could it be that his "wishful thinking" had actually worked?

Matthew shook his head. More likely Ms. White just hadn't wanted to stay after school herself. He remembered her checking her watch. Maybe she had a meeting to go to. Or a doctor appointment—she *had* seemed kind of tired. What if she was coming down with the flu or something? Poor Ms. White. He wished he didn't always make her so unhappy.

Matthew was so lost in thought, he almost didn't see Rebecca coming toward him. When he did, he jumped behind a tree to hide.

Rebecca Ram was a big bully, and she'd been in Matthew's class since kindergarten. In first grade she'd sat behind him in class, and pinched his neck till he let her borrow his crayons. They were always broken when he got them back. And last year she'd slugged him in the stomach the one time he actually beat her at wall-ball. Fortunately she was absent a lot.

Since Rebecca hadn't been in school today, Matthew wondered what she was doing outside. His mom always made him stay indoors if he was sick. "If you're well enough to play outside, you're

well enough to go to school" was her motto.

Matthew peeked from behind his tree. Rebecca was getting closer and closer. The way she walked, swinging her arms, reminded him of gorillas he'd seen at the zoo. Come to think of it, Rebecca kind of *looked* like a gorilla too, with her shaggy dark brown hair and squashed-up nose. As he watched, she turned and seemed to look straight at him!

Matthew ducked. His heart was thumping. If Rebecca had seen him, he was dead meat. He squeezed his eyes shut. *Don't beat Matthew up. Don't beat Matthew up*, he thought at her.

When he opened his eyes, Rebecca had passed him!

Matthew waited till Rebecca disappeared around a corner before leaving the safety of the tree. Then he ran the rest of the way to Daniel's house.

When he rang the doorbell, Mrs. Dobson, Daniel's mom, answered the door. "Oh, hi, Matthew," she said. "I haven't seen you in a while."

"Well, I've been kind of busy," Matthew said, not wanting to explain about having to stay after school, or that Daniel hadn't asked him to play that much lately.

"I'm afraid Daniel's not here," Mrs. Dobson said now. "He and Tim and Jess went to the video arcade at the mall. Jess's dad drove them after school."

"Oh." Matthew frowned. "I thought they were coming here to play ball."

"Maybe that was an earlier plan," Mrs. Dobson said.

"Maybe," said Matthew. Then he remembered something. "Don't you and Daniel have to go somewhere this afternoon?"

Mrs. Dobson looked puzzled. "No. Why would you think that?"

Matthew shrugged. "Never mind. I guess I'm just mixed up."

Chapter Three

Matthew's Fortune

As he walked home, Matthew was puzzled. In spite of what he'd told Mrs. Dobson, he hadn't been mixed up about what Daniel had said. He was only mixed up about why Daniel had said it! Why would Daniel ask him to play ball if he was planning on going to the video arcade?

When Matthew arrived home, his little sister, Sarah, met him at the door with a cookie in her hand. Sarah loved cookies.

"Mmm," said Matthew. "Chocolate chip. My favorite." He made a pretend grab for Sarah's cookie.

"Noo!" squealed Sarah. "*My* cookie!"

"Can't I have just one bite?" Matthew teased. "I'd share with you."

"Noo!" yelled Sarah. "Mine!" Only two and a half, Sarah was not very good at sharing. Especially when it came to cookies.

Matthew patted her curly blond head. "You can keep your old cookie. I don't want it anyway. It's got cooties on it."

Sarah studied her cookie. "Where cooties?" she asked.

Matthew laughed. "You can't see them; they're invisible. But don't worry. They taste just like chocolate chips."

Sarah took a bite of her cookie. "Mmm. Cooties good!"

That evening Matthew and his family drove to the Hing Ho Chinese restaurant for dinner. As they slid into a booth, a boy with close-cut black hair and thick glasses waved at Matthew from a table across the room.

Matthew smiled and waved back.

"Who's that?" his mom asked. "Someone from school?"

Matthew nodded. "Adam Lewis. He's new this year." Matthew didn't know Adam very well. He seemed like a nice kid, but he was kind of quiet, and his desk was at the opposite side of the room from where Matthew sat.

After they'd polished off the pork chow mein and most of the broccoli beef and fried rice, the waiter brought a plate of fortune cookies.

Matthew cracked his open and unfolded the paper slip inside. It read: YOU HAVE THE POWER TO INFLUENCE PEOPLE. USE IT WISELY.

Oh sure, thought Matthew. But the very next moment he remembered what had happened at school with Ms. White—how she'd let him go without his doing his home-work. And then he remembered how Rebecca had passed right by him after he'd sent her the message about not beating him up.

Rebecca might not have seen him, of course, but what if she had, and the fortune cookie was right? What if he really did have the power to influence people?

While his dad left the table to pay their bill, and his mother spooned leftover rice and broc-coli beef into cartons to take home, Matthew watched Sarah nibble at her fortune cookie. Suddenly he had an idea. He squeezed his eyes shut. *Give Matthew the cookie. Give Matthew the cookie,* he thought.

Matthew opened his eyes. Sarah was watching

him. "Here," she said, thrusting her cookie at him. "*Maffew's* cookie."

Wow! Sarah would never give up a cookie of her own free will. He could do it! Matthew had sent Sarah a thought message, and she had received it. He really did have the power to influence people, to get them to do what he wanted. Only he didn't actually want Sarah's cookie. It was just a test.

Sarah waved her cookie under Matthew's nose. "Take!" she yelled.

Matthew eyed the cookie. "No thanks." The corner Sarah had been nibbling on was all gooey.

Sarah pressed the cookie to Matthew's mouth. "Me share!"

Matthew's mother looked up as she dropped the cartons of leftovers into a paper bag. "Isn't that sweet. Sarah's learning to share. Let's encourage her."

"But I don't want her cookie," Matthew protested.

Sarah frowned. "One bite!" she yelled.

"Okay, okay," said Matthew. Obviously his power was stronger than he'd thought. Sarah wasn't going to be happy till he followed through on his message.

Carefully Matthew bit off a piece of cookie that was mostly dry. From now on he'd have to be careful how he used his power. He'd have to make sure he only used it for what he really wanted.

When Matthew got home from the restaurant, he ran upstairs to his room. He took out a piece of paper and a pencil. At the top of the paper he wrote: WAYS TO USE MY POWER TO INFLUENCE.

Matthew chewed on the end of his pencil while he thought for a minute. Finally he drew a line down the paper, dividing it into two columns. He labeled the first column PEOPLE TO INFLUENCE, and the second column WHAT I WANT. Then he began to write.

PEOPLE TO INFLUENCE	WHAT I WANT
MOM AND DAD	A BIGGER ALLOWANCE, A LATER BEDTIME, NO CHORES
DANIEL	BE FRIENDS LIKE WE USED TO BE
REBECCA RAM	LEAVE ME ALONE!!
MS. WHITE	BETTER GRADES, NO HOMEWORK

Matthew stopped writing to read over his list. His power to influence would have to be super-strong for his parents to give him a bigger allowance. When it came to money, his parents were real tightwads. They even smuggled home-popped popcorn into movie theaters rather than pay for theater popcorn, which they said was overpriced.

Matthew read through the rest of his list. When he got to Ms. White, the word "homework" caused something in his brain to flicker. Homework? Oh no! He had *two* assignments due tomorrow. But with his new power, he didn't *need* to do them, did he? Matthew thoughtfully chewed on his pencil. Could he really count on his power to stop the homework assignments?

There was a lot he didn't know about his power, Matthew realized. Where had it come from, for example? And how long would it last? What if he woke up in the morning and his power was gone?

To be on the safe side, perhaps he'd better do the homework, at least for tonight. Ms. White would sure be pleased if he did. Remembering how tired she'd seemed that afternoon, Matthew thought he'd like to make her happy for once.

Chapter Four

Strange Happenings

The next day, as soon as he got to class, Matthew handed Ms. White his homework. With luck it'd be the last he'd have to do.

Ms. White's eyes widened. "You did your homework?"

Matthew was confused. He thought she'd be expecting it. He hadn't sent her the no-homework message yet. "Wasn't I supposed to?" he asked.

Ms. White nodded and smiled. "I'm just surprised, that's all." She patted Matthew on the shoulder. "I'm proud of you, Matthew. I hope you'll keep up the good work."

I may not need to after today, thought

Matthew. But he was glad he'd made Ms. White smile.

As Matthew walked to the back of the room to hang up his jacket, he passed Adam. Remembering last night, Matthew paused to say hi.

Adam shoved back his glasses and smiled shyly. "You use chopsticks pretty well."

Matthew grinned. "Thanks." He'd noticed that Adam's whole family used chopsticks—even his little brother, who couldn't have been much older than Sarah. But then Adam's family probably used chopsticks more than Matthew's family did: Adam's mother looked like she might be Chinese.

"See you later," Matthew said.

Adam smiled again and went to sit down.

Matthew continued on to the coat racks and hung up his jacket. He didn't see Rebecca coming until it was too late. She planted herself directly in front of him. "Hi," she said.

Rebecca was wearing jeans and a T-shirt with a picture of a scowling man on it. The words above and below the man said GO AHEAD. MAKE MY DAY!

Matthew shuddered. "Uh, h-hi, yourself," he stuttered. He tried to squeeze past her, but Rebecca thrust out an arm, blocking his escape. "What's your hurry?" she asked in her gravelly voice. She made a fist with her other hand, like she was getting ready to slug him.

"N-no hurry," said Matthew. Thinking fast, he said, "Th-that's a nice shirt you're wearing."

Matthew couldn't believe what happened next. Slowly Rebecca's fist unfolded. Dropping both arms, she looked down at her shirt. "You like it?"

"Uh, sure." Matthew gulped. "It's like . . . it's like a joke, see? This man is saying he wants you to do something nice for him, you know, make his day, but you can tell by his face that he doesn't really mean it."

Rebecca smiled strangely. Then, before Matthew could do anything to stop her, she kissed him on the cheek and ran off.

Chapter Five

The Power of Thought

Dazed, Matthew stumbled to his seat and sat down.

"What's the matter with you?" Daniel asked. "You're acting like a zombie."

Matthew shook his head to clear it. "I'm okay." He thought about asking Daniel why he'd invited him to his house yesterday when he wasn't even home, but decided to wait till later. He needed to think about what had just happened with Rebecca.

She had been planning to slug him. Matthew was sure of it. Had his comment about her T-shirt stopped her? Or could it be that the power of yesterday's thought message was still at work?

Don't beat Matthew up. But why had she kissed him? Just thinking about it made Matthew squirm. Even though it was probably too late, he rubbed her kiss off on his sleeve.

During math Matthew glanced up and saw Rebecca watching him from across the room. She smiled, then puckered her lips as if to kiss him again.

Yuck! Matthew looked away. His face felt warm. Had anyone seen what Rebecca had done? He certainly hoped not.

What was the matter with her, anyway? Matthew hadn't sent her a message to *like* him, only to not beat him up. Well, he'd send her a new thought message, that's what he'd do! Something to erase the power of the old message.

Matthew considered carefully how he should word it. Sending a message like *You hate Matthew* would take care of the kissing, but if his messages were as powerful as he thought, he'd wind up in a murder report on the news!

No, it would have to be something else. How about *Leave Matthew alone?* Like he'd written down last night. Yes, that was better. It should take care of both the kissing *and* the slugging. But before Matthew could shut his eyes and send the message, the bell rang, and everyone streamed outside to the playground.

Matthew saw Adam pause at the door, like he was waiting for Matthew. But Matthew stayed at his desk. He'd be safer there. Rebecca might try to catch him if he went outside! He'd try sending the new thought message from the classroom. Of course, there was no guarantee the message would reach Rebecca if she wasn't in the same room. Still, it was worth a try.

After the door closed, Matthew squeezed his eyes shut.

"Matthew?"

His eyes popped open. Ms. White stood beside his desk. "Your eyes were closed," she said. "Aren't you feeling well?"

Matthew blushed. "No, I'm just kind of tired, that's all." It was only a small lie.

Ms. White smiled. "Some fresh air and exercise might revive you. You'd better go outside."

"But . . . but I haven't finished my math." That at least was true. He'd been so busy worrying about "the Rebecca problem" that he'd only gotten half of his math done.

Ms. White cocked her head. "Matthew McGhee," she said, "this is a first. I can't believe you're *asking* to stay and finish your schoolwork." She laughed. "Get along now. I was planning to give the class some free time after recess to finish up assignments anyway."

Ms. White shooed Matthew outside. As the door closed firmly behind him, Matthew thought about the message he'd sent her yesterday. *Let Matthew go.* Obviously the message was still in effect.

Chapter Six

Complications

Matthew kept an eye out for Rebecca as he entered the playground. When he spied her shaggy head far out on the soccer field, he breathed a sigh of relief.

Sinking down down on a bench near the swings, Matthew tried to think. He wished he knew more about how his power worked. For instance, was there a limit to the number of thought messages he could send a person?

What if he was only allowed one message per person? Or what if the power of an old thought message had to wear off before he could send a new message? How long would that take? Could he cancel out an earlier thought message with a new thought? Matthew sighed. It was all so complicated! To find out more about his powers, he would have to experiment.

Matthew looked around to make sure no one was watching him. Then he squeezed his eyes shut. He pictured Ms. White in his mind and thought, *No homework for Matthew. No homework for Matthew.* Unless he had to be in the same room for Ms. White to receive his message, that should do it. Now he'd send a message to Rebecca.

Gritting his teeth, Matthew let her face float into his mind. *Leave Matthew alone. Leave Matthew alone*, he thought.

"What're you doing?" said a voice.

Matthew's eyes flew open.

Daniel grinned at him. "Too bad you couldn't play ball yesterday. Jess and Tim and I had a great time."

Matthew frowned. "Your mom didn't tell you I came by? She said you went to the mall to play video games."

For a second Daniel looked startled. Then he said, "That must've been *after* we played ball. Too bad we missed you. Maybe you could've come too."

Daniel was lying! But before Matthew could think what to say, the bell rang, and Daniel ran off to join Jess and Tim near the classroom door.

Matthew stared after him. Without warning, someone bumped into him from behind. A pair of hands that weren't his own covered his eyes. "Guess who?" said a gravelly voice.

Matthew's heart sank. He didn't have to guess. He tugged at Rebecca's hands to free himself.

"Bell rang," he told her. "Gotta go." But as he took a step away from her, toward the classroom, Rebecca grabbed his arm and spun him around till he faced her. "You're cute," she said. And before he could duck, she lunged at him, planting a kiss on his nose. Laughing, she ran ahead of him to the classroom. "See you later," she called over her shoulder.

Matthew cringed.

Chapter Seven

Message Madness

Back in the classroom Matthew tried to finish his math. But he couldn't stop wondering what had gone wrong with his thought message. Rebecca was supposed to leave him alone. He wished his power to influence had come with a set of directions. Hadn't Rebecca gotten the message? What if his power had simply disappeared as suddenly as it had come?

Matthew sucked on his pencil eraser. If his powers had really worn off, wouldn't Rebecca go back to beating him up? It seemed that his original message must still be in effect. What if he really *were* allowed only one thought message per person? Matthew shivered. If the old message never wore off, Rebecca might keep kissing him forever!

"Staying late after school again?"

Matthew jumped.

Daniel leaned over his side of the desk to point to Matthew's nearly blank math paper. "Boy, are you slow. I finished my math before recess."

Matthew shrugged. "I've been thinking about other things."

Daniel raised an eyebrow. "Like what?"

Matthew hesitated. Last year, when Daniel was his best friend, he could've told Daniel what was happening. And Daniel would've helped him too. But Daniel had changed. Still, who else could he tell? Matthew leaned toward Daniel. "Promise you won't tell anyone else?" he whispered.

Daniel rolled his eyes.

"I mean it," said Matthew. "I don't want anyone else to know."

"Okay, okay," said Daniel. He crossed his heart. "I promise."

Matthew took a deep breath. "I made Rebecca like me," he said in a low voice, "and now she won't leave me alone."

Daniel grinned. "Rebecca likes you?"

Matthew held a finger to his lips. "Shh. Not so loud. Let's go to the Conference Corner."

The Conference Corner was a quiet, private place in the left-hand corner of the classroom. Walled off on its two open sides by bookshelves and filing cabinets, you squeezed through a narrow gap to get to the inside, where there were a couple of comfortable beanbag chairs to sit in.

As long as you didn't go too often, or stay longer than five minutes at a time, you could go to the Corner to talk out a problem anytime Ms. White wasn't teaching. And Rebecca was definitely a problem.

Daniel and Matthew slipped through the opening and flopped into the beanbag chairs. "What do you mean you *made* Rebecca like you?" Daniel asked. "Why would you want to do that?"

Matthew sighed. "I didn't do it on purpose. I

just sent her a message to not beat me up. I didn't know it would make her start liking me."

Matthew picked at a hole in his jeans. "I tried sending her another message to leave me alone. But it didn't work. And now I can't get rid of the first message."

"Whoa," said Daniel. "What messages? You mean you sent her notes?"

"No," Matthew said. "Not *that* kind of message."

Daniel looked confused. "You e-mailed her?"

Matthew shook his head no.

Daniel threw up his hands. "What other kind of message is there?"

Matthew paused. Daniel was going to think he was crazy. Yet he'd said too much already to stop now. Matthew blew out a breath. "Thought messages."

Daniel's forehead wrinkled. "Thought messages?"

Matthew nodded. As quickly as he could, he explained to Daniel all that had happened since he'd first discovered his strange power to influence. It felt good to get it off his chest.

Daniel reddened a bit when Matthew told about arriving at Daniel's house early because Ms. White had let him go, but otherwise Daniel just listened, not saying a word.

"So now Gorilla-face is in love with you," Daniel said when Matthew had stopped talking.

Matthew almost laughed. He hadn't told Daniel he thought Rebecca resembled a gorilla. Matthew figured *he* was the only one who thought so. "What do you think I should do?" Matthew asked.

For a second Matthew could've sworn he saw a smile dart across Daniel's face, but then Daniel laced his fingers behind his head. "I'm not sure," he said with a frown.

"Oh." Matthew couldn't help feeling disappointed. He'd really hoped Daniel would know what to do.

Daniel leaned toward him. "Tell you what. I'll think about it tonight, and get back to you tomorrow. Okay?"

Matthew smiled. "Thanks." With Daniel on his side, things were sure to get better. Maybe he and Daniel would even become best friends again. It would be just like old times.

Chapter Eight

Scary Thoughts

After he and Daniel returned to their desks, Matthew worked hard to finish his math. At the end of the day Ms. White assigned spelling homework to the whole class. Matthew waited to see if she would tell him he didn't need to do it. But as he'd feared, neither of his new thought messages worked.

When the bell rang, Matthew shot out the classroom door ahead of Rebecca. If he could just keep away from her until tomorrow, everything would be okay. Daniel was smart. He was sure to come up with a plan. A plan that would return everything to normal. But in the meantime, Matthew turned back every few steps to make sure Rebecca wasn't following him.

Rebecca lived in the opposite direction, but who knew what she might do! Even as he ran up the steps to his own front door, Matthew glanced over his shoulder, half expecting Rebecca to pop up from behind a bush or something.

Matthew fumbled with the knob, then pushed open the front door. Sarah stood in the doorway. She was holding something behind her back. Smiling, she suddenly thrust out a whole fistful of gooey cookies. "Me share!"

Matthew fled to his room, and slammed his door shut. Who would've guessed that his power to influence would turn out to be a such a curse?

After dinner Matthew was loading the dishwasher when his mom said, "Your dad and I have been talking. We've decided that it's time we raised your allowance."

Matthew dropped the plate he'd been holding. It hit the floor and shattered into a thousand pieces.

"My fault!" his mom cried, grabbing the broom. "I guess it *is* quite a shock, your dad and I agreeing to part with money—especially since you didn't ask for it."

Matthew nodded, then stepped out of the way as his mom swept up the jagged pieces of glass. A bigger allowance was on his list, of course. And he'd been *planning* to send a message about it, but because of the problems he'd been having with his first two messages he hadn't done it yet! Was it possible he could send a message without really trying?

Matthew edged around the kitchen to fetch the dustpan, then held it down so his mom could sweep into it. "What made you decide to change my allowance?" he asked carefully.

Mom gave him a curious smile. "I would've thought you'd be more interested in knowing how much of a raise you're going to get."

"Oh, I am," Matthew said quickly. "I was just wondering, that's all."

Mom took the full dustpan and emptied it into the garbage under the sink. "The idea just came to us, I guess. You're getting older. You have more responsibilities. We just thought it was time."

The idea just came to us. Matthew gulped.

Handing him the dustpan to hold again, Mom said, "We were thinking maybe two more dollars per week. Does that sound about right to you?"

Matthew hesitated. "Uh, sure."

Mom raised an eyebrow. "You don't *sound* too sure. I guess we could make it three dollars more. But that's as much as we can afford."

"Two dollars is fine," Matthew said quickly. "Really." If he wasn't careful, he'd put his parents in the poorhouse, as his father was fond of saying whenever Matthew begged for expensive toys or games.

Mom gave him a funny look. "Okay then. We'll start your raise next week."

As soon as he could, Matthew escaped back to his room. He knew he should feel more excited about his raise. But the idea that he could send a thought message without even trying to was frightening. He'd have to be more careful to control his thoughts. But as soon as he thought about controlling his thoughts, his thoughts zoomed out of control.

He started thinking about how awful it would be if someone got hurt because of his thoughts. He saw a TV show once about a boy who hurt people that way. Of course Matthew wouldn't hurt anyone with his thoughts on purpose, but what if he got angry? A person could think all kinds of bad things when they were angry.

Matthew thought about how mad he'd felt a few weeks ago when Sarah sneaked into his room and broke apart a brand-new LEGO castle he'd spent hours putting together. He'd practically wanted to stuff those LEGO pieces down her throat!

Sarah was always getting into his stuff. Thinking about it now made Matthew feel angry all over again. He knew Sarah was only two and a half, but wasn't that old enough to know what's yours and what's someone else's? Mom and Dad ought to spank her when she did stuff like that.

"Whaaa!" Matthew jumped at the sound. Heart pounding, he rushed out of his room.

Sarah sat in the hallway between her room and his, sobbing.

"What happened?" Matthew asked frantically.

"Me hurt," Sarah said between sobs.

Matthew's stomach tightened. He'd made Mom and Dad spank her. It was all his fault!

Matthew picked Sarah up and hugged her. "I'm sorry. I'm sorry," he said over and over again.

Sarah stopped crying. She held out her little finger. "Kiss it," she commanded.

"Your finger? You hurt your finger?"

Sarah nodded.

Matthew examined the finger. It *did* look a little red.

"Kiss it," Sarah commanded again.

Relieved, Matthew did. "There," he said. "All better now." Life sure was a lot easier when you were only two and a half; a kiss could *solve* a problem instead of creating one!

That night Matthew had a horrible nightmare. He and Rebecca were getting married! At the wedding ceremony, as they stood before the minister, Matthew couldn't bring himself to say "I do." Rebecca slugged him till he did. At the reception Sarah kept feeding Matthew cookies. Meanwhile his mom and dad, dressed in rags, shoved bags of money at him, saying, "Take it. Please take it. It's everything we have, but it's yours."

Matthew woke up shuddering. He hoped Daniel had come up with a good plan. Matthew was counting on his help.

Chapter Nine

Broken Promises

Arriving at school, Matthew slipped past Ms. White, who stood in the doorway greeting students. Hurrying to his seat, Matthew accidentally plowed into Adam, knocking Adam's glasses to the floor.

"Oh my gosh!" yelled Matthew. "I'm sorry." He scrambled to pick up Adam's glasses, which fortunately hadn't broken.

Adam squinted as Matthew handed him the glasses. "It's okay," Adam said, slipping them on. "They're always falling off. Even when I don't get bumped."

"Well," said Matthew. "I'll see you later then." He was anxious to talk to Daniel. It was why he'd been hurrying in the first place.

But Daniel wasn't at their desk, or back at the coat racks, either.

Matthew hoped Daniel wasn't sick. He sure wouldn't mind if Rebecca was absent though. Remembering his dream, he thought, *What if she tries to kiss me on the lips?!*

Matthew opened his backpack. His spelling book was on top. Oh no! He'd forgotten to do his homework again. Matthew pulled out his book, and a piece of paper.

In the next second everything went dark. Matthew grabbed at the hands covering his eyes. "Guess who?" said a gravelly voice.

"Hi," Matthew said weakly.

Rebecca dropped her hands and stepped in front of him.

Matthew's mouth fell open. She was wearing a frilly red dress, and there was a matching red ribbon in her hair.

"How do I look *today*?" she asked.

Matthew gulped. "Nice." She *did* look kind of nice, in a girl sort of way. But that didn't change the fact that she was still Rebecca.

"Rebecca Ram," Ms. White called out. "Unless you want to be counted absent, you need to take your seat."

"See you at recess," Rebecca hissed in Matthew's ear.

Taking a couple of deep breaths to calm himself, Matthew watched her leave.

Then he heard laughter. Matthew turned toward the sound. Daniel, Jess, and Tim stood in a huddle around Tim's desk at the front of the room. Daniel motioned toward Matthew, then toward Rebecca's retreating back. The three boys cracked up again.

Matthew's face grew warm. Daniel had broken his promise. He'd told!

"Back to your seats, boys," said Ms. White.

Matthew hoped she'd count them absent.

Daniel slid into his seat beside Matthew. He grinned and tapped his head. "Been sending any more messages?"

Before Matthew could respond, Daniel went on. "Rebecca in a dress. Can you believe it? Looks like she's trying to be the *gorill-uh* your dreams." He slapped Matthew on the back. "Get it? *Gorill-a. Girl of?*"

"I got it," Matthew said coldly. "I just didn't think it was funny."

Daniel stared at Matthew. "What's the matter with you? Can't you take a joke?"

Matthew glared back. "You promised not to tell anyone. You promised to help me!"

"Hold on a second," Daniel said. "Tim and Jess aren't just *anyone*. They're my best friends. And I never said I'd help you, I said I'd *think* about it." He shrugged. "In fact, I have thought about it."

"And?" In spite of his anger Matthew still wanted to believe that Daniel could rescue him somehow.

Daniel grinned. "And I think you and Rebecca are made for each other." He laughed.

Ears burning, Matthew turned away. And to think he'd wanted Daniel back as his best friend. Even if he could send a thought message to make Daniel his friend, he wouldn't do it now. A friend is someone you can trust. Someone who doesn't break promises and lie to you. Daniel was not his friend.

Chapter Ten

Worse Yet

By midmorning everyone in class seemed to know about Matthew and Rebecca. Several kids, including Tim and Jess, walked by Matthew's desk making smooching noises when Ms. White was busy with a reading group.

Worse yet, kids had heard about Matthew's powers—though they obviously didn't believe he could do what he'd done. "Hey, Matthew," a boy named Patrick called out as the class went down the hall to PE. "Make the teacher think I'm sick, okay? I don't want to run laps today."

"Ouch!" said Tim. "Matthew made me stub my toe!"

As they reached the gym, Matthew felt a tap on his shoulder. Turning, Matthew was relieved to see it was Adam, and not Rebecca or Daniel or any of the kids who'd been teasing him.

Adam smiled sympathetically. "Keep ignoring them," he whispered. "Then the teasing won't last long."

"Thanks," Matthew whispered back. He supposed Adam must've had some experience with being teased. Maybe because of his thick glasses.

As if he'd read Matthew's thoughts, Adam gave his glasses a push. Then he said, "Don't worry. Rebecca liked *me* earlier this year. She doesn't like anyone for long."

Maybe so, thought Matthew, but this time Rebecca was acting under the influence of a powerful thought message.

At recess time Matthew tried to stay inside. "I haven't done my spelling homework," he told Ms. White.

But as he'd feared, she only smiled. "I'm sure you'll get it done this afternoon."

Matthew wished he'd never had any powers at all. If only things could go back to the way they were before this whole mess began! Suddenly Matthew had an idea. If he was right about the way his powers worked, his idea was bound to succeed. And it would fix everything. Unless . . .

Matthew dismissed his negative thoughts. His idea just *had* to work. But, unfortunately, he didn't have time to carry it out: Rebecca was lying in wait for him as he left the classroom.

"There you are!" she said, catching hold of his arm. Rebecca dragged him over to a bench beside the playground. Matthew pulled his lips inside his mouth. If his lips didn't show, she couldn't kiss them.

With an evil glint in her eye, Rebecca leaned toward him. Just then a red ball came flying through the air. *Plonk!* It hit Rebecca square in the back of the head.

"Ouch!" She jumped off the bench. "Who did that!" As she scanned the playground for the ball's owner, Matthew quickly squeezed his eyes shut. Crossing his fingers, he sent *himself* a message: *You have no power to influence. No*

*power at all. All your power is erased.
Everything is back to normal.*

Matthew opened his eyes. Rebecca was chasing
some little kid around the edge of the playground
toward the football field, waving the ball that had

hit her. Her dress billowed up as she ran. It was a good thing she was wearing shorts underneath.

Out on the football field Daniel, Tim, and Jess were playing ball. Running backward to catch a high pass that had sailed off the field onto the playground, Daniel couldn't see Rebecca. They were going to collide!

Matthew jumped up and ran toward them. "Watch out!" he yelled. But he was too late. Matthew skidded to a stop as Rebecca and Daniel crashed into each other and landed in a strip of dirt.

Chapter Eleven

Normal

Matthew watched as Daniel sat up, rubbing his shoulder. "Ow." Head down, Rebecca bent over her knee.

"You okay?" Daniel asked. Rebecca lifted her head, and Matthew's eyes widened. He couldn't believe it. Rebecca was crying!

Rebecca didn't seem to notice Matthew. She glared at Daniel through tear-streaked eyes. "Of course I'm not okay," she said, sobbing. "I skinned my knee. It hurts. And my dress is ruined!"

Daniel's face wore a worried frown. He was probably afraid Rebecca would get him into trouble with the recess teacher. "Look," Daniel said. "I'm sorry. It was an accident." He helped Rebecca to her feet.

Matthew stood back a little, hoping they wouldn't see him.

"Your dress is only a little dirty," Daniel said. "I don't think it's torn."

"It was brand-new!" Rebecca sobbed.

Daniel twisted his hands together. "I bet your mom can wash it."

"It'll have stains," Rebecca cried. "It won't look as pretty."

"Sure it will," Daniel said.

Rebecca stopped crying. "So you think my dress is pretty?"

"Uh, sure," Daniel said.

She shook her head from side to side. "Do you like my ribbon, too?"

Matthew watched Daniel squirm. He thought he knew just how Daniel was feeling. "It's great," Daniel said. "I like red."

"Know what?" Rebecca said, eyeing Daniel in the same way she'd eyed Matthew just minutes before. "You're kind of cute." Pursing her lips, she dove at Daniel.

"Aargh!" Daniel yelled. Dodging her kiss, he ran off.

Matthew couldn't help smiling.

"Hey!" Rebecca yelled, noticing Matthew at last. "How long have you been watching?"

Matthew stopped smiling. "Since you and Daniel crashed."

Rebecca's eyes narrowed. "Listen," she growled. "You tell anyone you saw me cry, and I'll pound your face in!"

Matthew struggled to keep from grinning. "Your secret's safe with me." Unlike Daniel, he *kept* his promises.

Rebecca grunted, then stormed off after Daniel.

Walking back to the classroom after the bell rang, Matthew felt light and happy. It was as if a big, black cloud had been hovering over him for the last three days, and it'd finally lifted.

Adam was waiting for him outside the classroom door. He grinned. "I saw Rebecca chasing Daniel," he said. "Looks like you're off the hook."

Matthew grinned back. "I think you're right." Then he and Adam cracked up.

"You should've seen the look on Daniel's face when he streaked past me," Adam choked out. "His face was so white I thought Godzilla was after him."

"Rebecca *is* Godzilla," Matthew sputtered.

"Hee hee," Adam giggled. "Isn't *that* the truth!"

A new thought occurred to Matthew. "Hey," he said as they entered the classroom. "Would you like to play over at my house sometime?"

Adam smiled. "You bet!"

Matthew held out his hand, and he and Adam gave each other high fives.

At the end of the day Ms. White came by Matthew's desk. "Finished your spelling homework?" she asked.

Matthew slapped his forehead. With everything that had gone on that day, he'd forgotten all about the homework.

"I guess I'll take that as a 'no,'" Ms. White said dryly. "You'll need to stay after school and finish it."

Matthew could've *hugged* her for this final proof that his powers were gone. "Thank you, Ms. White. Thank you so much," he said. "I promise I'll get right on it."

Frowning, Ms. White seemed about to say something more, but then she turned and went back to her desk.

Matthew breathed a sigh of relief. Everything was back to normal. No. Better than normal. And today was Friday! He'd call Adam tonight and invite him over tomorrow. They could play video games, or maybe go outside and play ball if the weather was nice. He'd have to find out what Adam liked to do.

Humming, Matthew picked up a pencil and got to work.

AUTHOR BIO

Suzanne Williams has often engaged in wishful thinking but has yet to master the art of controlling other people's minds, much less her own. She lives in Renton, Washington, with her husband, two nearly grown children, and two dogs. The author of the Children's Choice Award–winning picture book *Library Lil*, this is her lucky thirteenth book for children. You can visit Suzanne on the Web at www.suzanne-williams.com.